THE CHICKEN SQUAD

A BACKYARD PET

By Doreen Cronin
Illustrated by Stephen Gilpin

Ready-to-Read

Simon Spotlight

New York   London   Toronto   Sydney   New Delhi

For Johnny and Buster
—D. C.
For Emmarie
—S. G.

SIMON SPOTLIGHT
An imprint of Simon & Schuster Children's Publishing Division
1230 Avenue of the America, New York, New York 10020
This Simon Spotlight edition August 2022
Text copyright © 2022 by Doreen Cronin
Illustrations copyright © 2022 by Stephen Gilpin
All rights reserved, including the right of reproduction in whole or
in part in any form. SIMON SPOTLIGHT, READY-TO-READ, and
colophon are registered trademarks of Simon & Schuster, Inc.
For information about special discounts for bulk purchases, please contact
Simon & Schuster Special Sales at 1-866-506-1949 or business@simonandschuster.com.
Manufactured in the United States of America 0723 LAK
10 9 8 7 6 5 4 3 2
CIP data for this book is available from the Library of Congress.
ISBN 978-1-6659-0617-3 (hc)
ISBN 978-1-6659-0616-6 (pbk)
ISBN 978-1-6659-0618-0 (ebook)

Sugar wakes up very late.
The sun is bright, and the
chicken house is empty.
"Where is everybody?" asks Sugar.
"They are playing in the yard," says
Moosh.

Sugar wants to play in the yard too.
She looks for her brother,
Poppy, to play with her.

Poppy is not in the chicken house.
He is not in the doghouse.
He is not under the picnic table
in his big shoe.

Sugar finds Poppy in the garden.
"Come play with me," says Sugar.

"Later," says Poppy.
"I am taking care of my pets."

"Flowers are not pets," says Sugar.
"Flowers are flowers."

"Flowers are beautiful," says Poppy.
"I take care of them,
and they make me happy."

"Flowers don't do anything!" says
Sugar. "Pets have to do something!"

"Flowers grow, and they sway in the
breeze," says Poppy.
"Flowers are great backyard pets!"

Sugar does not want to play
in the garden with pet flowers.
She looks for her sister Dirt.

Dirt is not in the chicken house.

She is not in the doghouse.

She is not inside the tire swing,
writing poems.

Sugar finds Dirt in a hole
by the fence.
"Come play with me," says Sugar.

"Later," says Dirt.
"I am watching my pets!"

Sugar looks in the hole.

"Worms are not pets," says Sugar.
"Worms are worms."

"They are busy all day long,"
says Dirt.

"And I love watching them.
Worms are great backyard pets."

Sugar does not want to be
in a hole with pet worms.
She looks for her sister Sweetie.

Sweetie is not in the chicken house.

She is not in the doghouse.

She is not paddleboarding
in the birdbath.

Sugar finds Sweetie running
along the bushes.

"Play with me," says Sugar.
"Later," says Sweetie.
"I am playing with my pet."

"Bushes are not pets!" yells Sugar.

"Not the bush," says Sweetie.
"The butterfly!"

"His name is Lenny," Sweetie says.
"And we play together every day.
Sometimes I chase Lenny.
Sometimes Lenny chases me.
Butterflies are great backyard pets!"

Sugar looks at Poppy in the garden
with his pet flowers.

Sugar looks at Dirt in the hole
with her pet worms.

Sugar looks at Sweetie
chasing her pet butterfly.

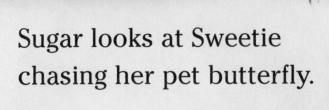

Sugar visits J.J. in the doghouse.
He is asleep.
Sugar wakes him up.

He does not sway in the breeze.
He refuses to dig a hole.
He will not chase her.
"Dogs are terrible pets!"
Sugar says.

Sugar lies down
in the soft, tall grass.

She watches the clouds drift by.
They are beautiful.
They are busy moving across the sky.
One of them looks like a dinosaur.

Poppy, Dirt, and Sweetie find Sugar in the grass.

"Are you ready to play?" they ask.

"Later," says Sugar.

"I'm playing with my clouds."

"They're beautiful," says Poppy, "and they float on the breeze!"
"Look how busy they are!" says Dirt.
"We should chase them!" says Sweetie.

"Clouds are great pets," says Sugar.
"I hope they come back tomorrow!"